To Emma,

Thank you for your unwavering support and endless love.

Duane.

Little Chalico was very small, standing at only three feet tall.

What he lacked in height he made up in heart and this is what set him apart.

Over dinner one evening his father sat by his side.
"You will soon be a man" said his father with pride.

Chalico said "But I'm not tall, I cannot be a warrior, I am too small."

His father smiled, his eyes very wise and to little Chalico this was a surprise.

"It's not what you look like or how strong you may be."
It's the strength on the inside that really counts, you see."

"You may be small but it has been foretold."

"You will be brave. You will be bold."

Next day Little Chalico went for a stroll, meeting his friends by the tall totem pole.

Soon they were teasing him about his size, saying he was no taller than an eagles thighs.

They carried on calling Chalico names, thinking it was just fun and games.

"You are too small to use your bow and the arrows fly way too slow."

"You will be too scared to use your axe, you would be no good if a wolf attacks."

"If the spirits have their way, you will hide in your tipi all night and day."

As anger lines crossed Chalico's brow, he turned to his friends and made his vow.

"I am braver than you all, but for me to prove this we will not brawl."

"I will go to the ghost town on my own, following the path the crows have flown."

"There I will face my biggest fears and confront the Wasichu spirit if it appears."

Mounting his horse he turned to see, the sun beating down and the crows flying free.

Heading to the ravine the mighty river flowed, passing the totem pole little Chalico rode.

Out of the village passing Eagles Crag is where little Chalico met his first snag.

"Hello little Chalico where do you ride?"

The bison stood solid and fast.

"This far from home you need a guide."

"Maybe I should not let you past."

"Strong bison let it be known."
"I am going to the ghost town all alone."
"I am brave, I am bold."
"So I've been told, so I've been told."

And so on he rode. . .

"Hello little Chalico where do you go?"

The snake appeared from under a boulder.

"Come with me I have something to show."

As he prepared to bite Chalico's shoulder.

"Slippery snake retreat under your stone."
"I am going to the ghost town all alone."
"I am brave, I am bold."
"So I've been told, so I've been told."

And so on he rode. . .

"Hello little Chalico you look weary."

The vulture eyed his next meal.

"Come rest those eyes that look so bleary."

"Do we have a deal?"

"Hungry vulture let your belly groan."
"I am going to the ghost town all alone."
"I am brave, I am bold."
"So I've been told, so I've been told."

And so on he rode. . .

Perched up high at the top of the ravine, looking down at the river and the breathtaking scene.

Following its path meandering down, little Chalico saw the outline of the town.

Onwards he rode wondering what he may find, nightmarish images ran through his mind.

Pushing the visions out of his head, he repeated the words his father had said.

"I am brave, I am bold."

"So I've been told, so I've been told."

At the towns edge something startled his horse, was it the Wasichu supernatural force?

Turning fast Chalico let out a sigh as a tumbleweed rolled and trundled by.

Summoning his courage and maintaining his course, knowing a tumbleweed was the source.

He urged on his horse towards the challenge ahead, still repeating the words his father had said.

"I am brave, I am bold."

"So I've been told, so I've been told."

Through the main street each step taken with care, riding his horse as fast a he dare.

Movement from the corner of his eye and this time it was not a tumbleweed rolling by.

In a far off window a shadowy figure stirred, a sinister presence was surely absurd.

On closer inspection it turned out to be, a musty old curtain blowing free.

Chalico rode on, his tummy full of dread, repeating the words his father had said.

"I am brave, I am bold."

"So I've been told, so I've been told."

At the saloon Chalico dismounted his horse, the sun was high and it's heat no remorse.

He pushed open the saloon door, rays of sunlight hit the floor.

The wood floor creaked beneath his feet, he was pleased to be out of the blistering heat.

The feeling he had did not long stay, as the dust settled his smile slipped away.

Not letting in fear he focused instead on repeating the words his father had said.

"I am brave, I am bold."

"So I've been told, so I've been told."

Heading towards the back of the room, his eyes struggled in the darkened gloom.

Then out of the darkness emerged a sight, the likes of which gave him a fright.

He had no words for what he saw and very nearly ran out of the door.

A tall pale figure that made no sound, it was time little Chalico stood his ground.

"I am brave, I am bold."

"So I've been told, so I've been told."

Neither figure made a move, both seemed to have something to prove.

The spirit trembled and the sound it made, was a high pitched shriek which began to fade.

When the sound had stopped and was no more, the figure crashed to the floor!

Chalico jumped back but to his surprise, he saw three pairs of feet and three pairs of thighs.

He pulled the sheet with a heavy yank, revealing his friends playing their prank.

His friends laughed loudly filled with glee, "Your face!" one said with a hand on his knee.

"I wasn't scared" said Chalico, "I am brave, I am bold, I told you so."

Then out of the corner came a sound, "What are you doing here?" something growled.

They turned their heads and what did they see; a ghost at a table drinking whiskey.

Chalico's friends turned and fled, Chalico stayed filled with dread.

"Your friends have gone, but you have not, you are braver than the lot."

"Come join me for a drink and see, there's no reason to be scared of me."

Chalico sat but before he spoke the ghost vanished leaving only smoke.

Then from nowhere came a voice, "Not many would sit given the choice".

"Now go and tell your friends of old, that you are brave and you are bold."

Out of the gloom and into the light, Chalico saw his friends still pale from fright.

"You ran" he said, "you were scared". They looked at each other not saying a word.

They mounted their horses and rode into the sun, "You fell off a stool" said Chalico poking fun.

The laughter started between all three, it was clear who the bravest now must be.

His friends then agreed that stories told would be of "Chalico, the brave and bold."

First published 2019.

ISBN-13: 978-16864113902

Copyright: James Fenwick & Duane Nunn.

Other titles authored by James Fenwick and illustrated by Duane Nunn.

The Paper Dragon

The Bothy Ghost

Printed in Great Britain
by Amazon